The Rabbi and the
Twenty-nine Witches

The Rabbi and the Twenty-nine Witches

a Talmudic legend

retold and illustrated by MARILYN HIRSH

Holiday House · New York

Library of Congress Cataloging in Publication Data

Hirsh, Marilyn.
  The rabbi and the twenty-nine witches.

  SUMMARY: A wise old rabbi finally rids the
village of the witches that terrorize it every
night that the moon is full.
  [1. Folklore, Jewish]   I. Title.
PZ8.1.H66Rab   [398.2]   [B]   75-30710
              ISBN 0-8234-0270-3

Once there was a little village where people were neither rich nor poor, good nor bad, wise nor foolish, except for the Rabbi who was very wise. In this little village children went to school, cows gave milk, and grown-ups worked.

It was a very normal village except that under a nearby hill, in a deep, dark cave, there lived twenty-nine of the meanest, scariest, ugliest, wickedest witches that ever were.

There they lived and there they stayed, brewing their evil potions and raising their evil bats and buzzards. They practiced zooming around on broomsticks and screeching their hideous screeches. They pulled the tails of their cats and bit each other out of sheer nastiness. They turned flowers into poison mushrooms and planted them all around the cave.

But once a month, when the moon was full, the witches came out of their cave. They flew to the village and circled above it, shrieking and howling and laughing their horrible laughs. The cats yowled, the dogs yelped, the chickens laid cracked eggs, and the cows gave sour milk. The babies cried and everyone else had terrible witchy nightmares. But if it was raining on the night of the full moon, the twenty-nine witches did not come at all.

Now the next time the moon was full and it was not raining, everyone came home early. They locked their doors and bolted their shutters. Some hid under the bed. Others put pillows over their heads to drown out the creepy screeches.

People got born, grew up, and died without ever seeing the full moon.

Finally one old grandmother said, "I want to see the full moon before I die! Is that too much to ask?"

"Well," said her friend, "considering the witches it is quite a bit. We will go to the Rabbi and he will know what to do. After all, he is the Rabbi." So they did.

The Rabbi thought and thought about the problem. On the day before the next full moon, he reasoned, "If there is no full moon there are no witches, so there is no problem. But if there is a full moon there are witches and that is a problem. But if it rains on the night of the full moon there are no witches and there is no problem." He thought some more. "But if it rains on the night of the full moon there are no witches," he thought again. "That's it! I have a splendid idea," he cried out loud. "And I can try it out tomorrow night if the rain is still falling."

The Rabbi quickly called the grandmother to his side. "Have twenty-nine of the bravest men in the village come to me tomorrow night. Each one should bring a long white robe and a clay pot with a tight cover."

On the next night, as the rain was coming down, he said, "We are going to get rid of the twenty-nine witches once and for all. Put your robes carefully in the clay pots. Cover them tightly, for they must stay dry."

As brave as the men were, this was rather terrifying. But they trusted him for, after all, he was the Rabbi.

In the pouring rain they set out over the hills to the dark, dangerous witches' cave. Each one carried his pot with his dry white robe in it. By the time they got near the cave even the bravest one was scared. Some say that the Rabbi looked a little worried too.

They hid under a ledge near the cave. The Rabbi whispered, "I will go in first because, after all, I am the Rabbi. When I whistle once put on your robes. When I whistle again rush in and each of you pick up a witch. Start to dance with her. After that just listen to me." The Rabbi put on his long, dry, white robe and his most frightening expression and went into the cave.

"Witches, witches, I'm coming in," he cried.

"Whooo are youoooo?" they screeched.

"I'm one of youoooo," he cried.

He looked so scary that they said, "You do look like a witch but how did you stay so dry?"

"I walked between the raindrops," he said.

"What a trick," they cackled. "Doooo come in."

"Why have you come?" the chief witch scowled.

"Why not?" answered the Rabbi as bravely as he could. "You show me some magic and then I will show you some magic and we will all learn something."

"Why not?" said the witches.

So the Rabbi dared them to prepare him a wonderful feast.

One witch waved her wand and bread appeared. Another brought wine out of the air, and another brought fruit.

Soon there was a great table filled with plates and goblets, roasts and stews, cakes and cookies, soups and puddings, and every other good thing that there is to eat.

"So let's eat," said the Rabbi, forgetting for just a moment the reason he had come.

"Not so fast," said the chief witch. "Now show us some of your tricks."

"Ah yes," said the Rabbi slowly. "For my first trick I will produce twenty-nine handsome young men to dance with you at the banquet."

"That is quite a trick," cackled the witch. "No one has asked me to dance in four hundred years."

The Rabbi whistled once and waited a minute. He whistled again and in rushed the brave men. Each grabbed a witch and started to whirl her around.

"And now for my greatest trick of all," cried the Rabbi. "I'll teach you to dance between the raindrops. Everyone outside."

The men picked up the witches and carried them off into the rain.

"Youooooo tricked us," shrieked the witches in hissing, horrible, shrinking shrieks. For the Rabbi had figured out that witches must be afraid of the rain for a very good reason. As the men watched in amazement, the witches became smaller and smaller until they completely shrank away into nothing.

"It shouldn't happen to our worst enemies," said the men, for it was a sad sight to see.

But a good feast should not go to waste. So someone ran back to tell the people in the village that the witches were gone forever. Everyone came and danced and ate.

And on the night when the moon was full, all the people in the village from the oldest grandmother to the youngest baby came out to look. The cool, soft light turned the rooftops to silver. They all agreed that the full moon was very beautiful. When they had looked and looked for a long time everybody felt sleepy. So they went back to their houses and got into their beds and went to sleep. And nobody had any nightmares.